J. Burgess

Memorandum on the Remains

J. Burgess

Memorandum on the Remains

ISBN/EAN: 9783337385460

Printed in Europe, USA, Canada, Australia, Japan

Cover: Foto ©Andreas Hilbeck / pixelio.de

More available books at **www.hansebooks.com**

Archæological Survey of Western India.

MEMORANDUM

ON

THE REMAINS

AT

GUMLI, GOP, AND IN KACHH, &c.,

BY

J. BURGESS, F.R.G.S., M.R.A.S., M. DE LA SOC. AS.,

ARCHÆOLOGICAL SURVEYOR AND REPORTER TO GOVERNMENT.

Bombay:

PRINTED BY ORDER OF GOVERNMENT AT THE GOVERNMENT CENTRAL PRESS.

1875.

ARCHÆOLOGICAL SURVEY OF WESTERN INDIA.

Edinburgh, 18*th June* 1875.

Tʜᴇ CHIEF SECRETARY ᴛᴏ GOVERNMENT,

Bᴏᴍʙᴀʏ.

Sɪʀ,

In continuation of the Memorandum No. 2, submitted to Government some time ago, and detailing the operations of the Archæological Survey till the end of January last, I have the honour to submit the following outline of the survey during the months of February, March, and part of April.

Gᴜᴍʟɪ. The temple known as Naulâkhâ stands on a raised platform 153½ ft. long by 102 ft. broad. The enclosing wall or screen on the top of this, however, has entirely disappeared ; and of the entrance only the steps and the bases of the two massive pillars above them remain. The temple itself measures 51 ft. 5 in. from the threshold of the *mandap* to that of the shrine, and 67 ft. 8 in. to the back of the *pradakshina* inside. The width from the north to the south doors of the mandap is 55 ft. 7 in. The level of the temple is considerably raised above that of the court, and is approached by a flight of steps at each of the three doors. The mandap is of two storeys, with twenty-two columns on the floor, each 9 ft. 7 in. high, and thirty shorter ones on the low screen walls that enclose it. It is of a pretty common cruciform shape, the central area being 29 ft. square ; to each side of this an aisle is added 19 ft. long, except on the west side, where in front of the shrine it is only 15 ft. 7 in. long ; outside this on the three outer sides is added a portico about 8¼ ft. square.

The shrine is 9 ft. 1 in. square inside, and is roofed by a neat dome with *chakwâs* on the lintels of the octagon. The linga that once occupied it was carried off to Porbandar long ago, and is now to be seen there in the temple of Kedar-nâth.

Round the shrine is a *pradakshina* about 3 ft. wide, but widening to over 5 ft. opposite the windows that on the different sides throw light into it.

The walls of this temple are built of slabs of moderate size of the calcareous sandstone so common over Western Kâthiawâd, and are set on edge and clamped together. This mode of construction has hastened the ruin of this stately pile ; for, the walls being thin, when once a tree or plant has got its roots in between the slabs, it has split the wall. In many of the stones there are small natural cavities which when exposed have been occupied by plants that at first sight seem to grow out of the solid stone.

The central octagon of the *mandap* supports a frieze, with a low parapet wall above in front of the gallery or upper floor, to which there does not appear to have been any regular means of access, unless it may have been by means of some wooden ladder. The dome rests on the columns of this second storey, but the pendentive and some of the upper courses of stone have fallen in, and it is now open in the centre. This *mandap* is what Captain (now Sir G.) LeGrand Jacob described in 1837 as "the palace". With the exception of this strange mistake, however—and unscientific observers seem to have a sort of fatality for glaring mistakes—his account generally conveys a very accurate idea of this temple: being much better than Colonel Tod's in 1822.

The brackets of the columns both in the upper and lower floors are sculptured, each with a different device consisting of *kirtimukhs*, or *grásdás*, the *gatachuk*, four-armed figures, a bird trimming its feathers, an elephant or an elephant's head, a large human face, a monkey—two with one head, a bird with a flower in its beak, a horse with a man before and another behind, a pair of bullocks butting, an elephant and horse, a cock and sheep, a swordsman and elephant, a pair of birds, a couple of fishes, three monkeys, &c.[*]

The columns of the octagon and four in front of the shrine have bases of the broken-square plan, with a figure of a Devî having the left foot raised on the right knee, placed in a small compartment the colonnettes on each side which have the *grásdá* or griffon attached as a bracket to the outward sides. Over this are horizontal mouldings to a height of 2 ft. 3 in. The next division is 1 ft. 8 in. high, and has a standing figure of a *devata*, Ganpati, S'iva, Pârbati, &c. &c., on each face. Over this is more ornamentation, and the column changes to an octagon, on the sides of which are carved eight *Devîs* as on the base, only somewhat smaller. At 5 ft. 11 in. from the floor the pillars become circular and are girt, first by a collar of sixteen leaves and buds, then by a string of *chakwás*,—hanging by eight short bands from a cincture of lozenge-shaped carvings, over which is a belt, about 8 in. deep, of 8 kirtimukhs. The capital is 9 inches deep[†] and the bracket 13½ inches. The other ten columns are much plainer.[†]

The carving on the outside is what has chiefly attracted attention to this temple. On each face of the base of the shrine or *vimana*, under the windows, are two elephants and a *makar* or *grásdá* with their trunks intertwined. On the upper members of the base are—1, a line of kirtimukhs ; 2, elephants holding a band or rope in their trunks, their ears just touching, and at the outer angles a human figure struggling as if to keep the rope off from him ; and, 3, a line of figures, mostly human, dancing, kneeling, playing music, fighting, &c. &c., with elephants, horses, linga, altar, a pair of intertwined snakes, birds, figures sitting on chairs, &c. &c., intermixed. Above this the first belt of the walls is occupied with figures of Devî or Lakshmî, four-armed, with the left foot raised as on the pillars of the mandap. Over this is a dorus and some mouldings ; then the principal belt, as at Ambarnâth and elsewhere, filled with larger figures, principally gods and goddesses of the S'aiva mythology—some of the figures tolerably well executed, and the females without the usual exaggerations.[‡] The brackets sup-

---

[*] A few sketched : more might have been drawn had the assistant exerted himself.
[†] Drawings made.
[‡] One drawn, and photographs taken.

porting these have each a flower carved on the under side, with two leaves. Each compartment is enclosed by a pair of colonnettes, with brackets of the goat-shaped or griffon figure with long legs, and horns. The figures in the receding portions and re-entrant angles are all males, or nearly so, and have beards of the formal cut so common on Rájput sculptures and on the figures Mr. Sherring styles ' Bhar' ; some have also moustaches, and occasionally a turban badly set on. Indeed, until within a century ago or so, turbans are not usual on Hindu sculpture, and such as do exist are represented rather *over* the head than *on* it. Close above these last are two very small figures on a sort of shelf. Above this belt is a cornice, of which monkeys crown all the corners. Among the minor sculptures on this temple are some obscene figures, but not many : on a Vaishṇava temple they would probably have been a characteristic feature.

Under the shrine window on the south side, and just over the two elephants, is a figure of Brahma and Sarasvatî ; in the corresponding position on the west is S'iva and Parvatí ; on the north the figures are completely destroyed,—they were probably Vishṇu and S'rí.*

Over the porches have been slabs with human and animal figures, but they have nearly all fallen. The other compartments of the roofs have lotuses or other circular flowers carved upon them.

Heaps of stones lie about, many of them elaborately sculptured.†

To the south-west of this temple, and only a few yards from the outer en-closure of it, is the *s'ikhar*, or spire, of what Tod calls " the temple of wisdom," or of Ganpati ; and Captain Jacob—that of Hanuman : it is now so utterly ruined that no one can say to whom it was dedicated. Nothing remains of it but the *vimana*, or tower, bereft of the jambs and lintel of the door, and three or four pillars of the maṇḍap. But the style of this tower is of an old type :‡ it measures 7 ft. 9 in. square inside, and the walls are 2 ft. 3 in. thick, but, unlike the Naulákhá, the stones are smaller, very carefully jointed and laid on their beds. The mode of closing the spire, too, is the same as that of the Son Kansârî temples on a hill above, to be described presently.

A little to the east of this is the Wâniâwasi—the ruin of an old Jaina temple, of which only a few pillars of the maṇḍap and three of the small cells that surrounded it now remain :—scarcely sufficient, without turning over a large por-tion of the fallen stones, to determine the plan and dimensions. The pillars are plain, but the bracket capitals have the same whimsical variety of sculpture as those of the Naulákhá Temple. The doors of the little shrines of the bámtí, or court, have been elaborately carved in sandstone.

Among the stones was found an image of Pârswanâth carved in a hard yellowish stone of great specific gravity : it is about 4 ft. high, and but little damaged.‡

---

* These notes very imperfectly describe the sculptures, which will be better illustrated by four photographs taken of them.
† A group of them was photographed.
‡ Photographed.
ꞏ 197—*b*

East of this, again, is the Jethâ Wâv, which must originally have been a large and noble public well ;* but half of it has entirely disappeared, and the stones carried off. On a slab on the right side near the entrance, or east end, under a cow and calf eating balls of food, is an inscription, of which only small fragments here and there are legible. It began :—

ૐ ॥ संवत् १३८१

probably Samvat 1383 =A.D. 1326-7—only three years before the traditional date of the destruction of the city.

At the bottom of the descent is a *goklde*, or niche, on each side, very neatly carved.

Of the Râmapola, or west gate, which was standing only a few years ago, and might then have been saved by a few props and cutting down the vegetation over it, only two of the brackets now remain, hanging over the ruin.* The gate, however, notwithstanding the praises it has received from visitors, was never probably equal to those at Dabhoi. It belonged to the same style and was of about the same dimensions, the walls being 13 feet apart, and the clear roadway between the pilasters 11 ft. 6 in.

Outside this gate are a few pâliyas still standing, and many more trampled into the earth by the cattle, while others have been carried off for building purposes. The figures carved on them are mostly represented on horseback—the horses covered with what may equally pourtray a thick quilt or chain-armour.

Just outside is the Derânî Wâv, a much smaller and plainer structure than the Jethî Wâv, and also much decayed.

Scattered about all over the site of Gumli are fragments of temples and other buildings ; but, so far as I could discover by visiting all I could catch a glimpse of over the jungle, or hear of from the villagers at Mukhânâ, there are no others worth special notice either for size or carving. They appear to have been mostly small shrines of the twelfth and thirteenth centuries, and now quite ruined.

Between the Râmapola and Mukhânâ in the valley to the east of the old city are the remains of several wells.

Ascending the gorge above Gumli, however, to the south-west, under some magnificent old mango trees, and commanding a splendid view of the Naulâkhâ and all the valley round it, are three old temples. Of the first—the shrine 5 ft. 1 in. square inside with walls 18 in. thick and a *pradakshina* 2 ft. 5 in. wide round it —stand. On the lintel of the shrine door is Ganes'a, and on the frieze above is Vishṇu seated, with Garuda below his *asana*, a nimbus behind his head and female figures at each side : to the left of Vishṇu in another compartment is Brahma, three-faced, seated cross-legged on two *naṅsas*, with two female attendants ; and to the right is S'iva—three-faced, with Nandi below, and two females. All three have four arms each, and are about 15 inches high. In front of the shrine door two pillars of the *maṅdap* still remain, divided into three nearly equal lengths of four, eight, and sixteen sides, with capitals of cruciform shape.

* Photographed.

The second temple, on the south side of the last, has had a mandap with low screen wall 1 ft. 9 in. thick. The shrine is 6 ft. 4 in. square inside, with walls 2 ft. 2½ in. thick, surrounded by a *pradakshina* 3½ ft. wide, the outer walls of the temple forming an oblong 17 ft. 4 in. by 29 ft. inside and 21 by 32½ ft. outside, with four pillars in front of the shrine, 2 ft. 2 in. square below, octagon above, and having square bases. They have round capitals and brackets of kirtimukhs and four-faced figures.

The walls are of plain ashlar, the stones neatly dressed and jointed. There has been a porch, but it has fallen.

The s'ikhar is much ruined, but has been carved with a sort of chaitya-window pattern, not deeply cut, and other mouldings usual in temples from the eighth century or earlier to the tenth or eleventh, and crowned with a large flat amlas'ila.

On the south side of this are three small cells occupied by a Káki Báwá, and beyond them is a large well, built of well-dressed stone.

On the very summit of the hill is a small square shrine of Asopurá Mátá, and near it the walls of many of the houses of the long-deserted fort, surrounded by a massive wall, of which the crenellations only have fallen.

Outside the Rámapola and to the south-west of the Derání Wáv is the remains of a pretty large artificial lake—the Salsánr Talño. At the east end of it is a small S'aiva temple, now a complete ruin, the mandap entirely fallen, and the shrine only remaining, much dilapidated about the s'ikhar. There is nothing, however, remarkable about it.

About 350 or 400 feet above this is another large talño—the Son Kansári, with some eighteen or twenty temples at the west end of it, and two or three at the east :—none of them very large, but all apparently of an earlier date than those below. The larger ones consist of a square shrine built near one end of an oblong court or mandap, and the smaller ones of an outer room or a porch and a cell. The mandaps have fallen, except that of one of the three larger ones, of which a considerable portion is still entire. This appears to have been a Vaishnava temple with four columns in the mandap. From the *pradakshina* a small door opens on the right or north side into a little room outside the enclosure wall, and at the back and south sides there are small openings or windows into similar apartments : these cells were probably for storing the clothing, jewels, and articles of value belonging to the idol. The roofs of the *pradakshina* and aisles in these temples have slanted downwards.

In the mandap of this last is a figure of Vishnu about 4½ ft. high, broken across the neck, but otherwise scarcely damaged. It would be worth removing to a local museum at Rájkot or even to Bombay. It was from these temples that Captain Jacob removed the figure of Brahma, now in the Asiatic Society's Museum at Bombay.

These shrines, however, differ from most others in the way they are roofed : the s'ikhar being gradually contracted in dimensions inside till it terminates in a square aperture of about a foot, covered by a single slab. In one of the larger temples, on the north side of this group, there appears to have been two floors, and above the second the area is gradually contracted in this way. This shrine is 10 ft. 9 in. square inside, and the walls 3 ft. 9 in. thick, with a *pradlakshina* 6 ft. wide, having four windows—one on each side and two behind.

At the east end of the talâo is a temple with a pretty large *naos* roofed over in a similar way, as is also its shrine. The walls are all built of carefully-squared stones laid on their beds, and probably built without lime, though, before they ceased to be used, they seem to have been pointed and white-washed.

Many carved stones, *piliyas*, images, &c., lie about.*

8th February.—Made an excursion to Sakrojâ Talâo, about nine miles off, but fully a third of the way was through jungle among the Bardâ Hills, where riding was impossible. It is a small artificial lake in the bosom of the hills, and has four shrines at the cardinal points. That on the south, facing east, seems to have been the principal one, and is the only one still used. The small mandaps of all of them have fallen, and the *vimanas* measure about 7 ft. 2 in. square outside. I found no inscription here.

Between three and four miles south of Mukhânâ is the Vikiya Wâv, which, with the *chattra* in front of it, is 216 feet in length.† The chattra or mandap at the east end is supported by twelve pillars, and measures 18 ft. 6 in. square. From this the steps descend to the wâv, which is 14 ft. 10 in. wide, and bridged over at intervals about 41 feet apart by three canopies,—at one end of each of which narrow stairs descend into the *wâv* and landing on the platforms below. The circular well at the west end is 18 ft. 8 in. in diameter, but the whole is filled up with earth to about the level of the first platform below the surface—about 12 feet down, and large banyan trees have taken root on the sides, which have been faced with 2 ft. 7 in. of stone in front of the rock out of which the whole has been hewn.

The style of the pillars, &c., is in keeping with that of the Naulâkhâ Temple : the same whimsical variety in the bracket figures is also very noticeable.

At Pâsthar, a little to the south, is an old temple to the sun-god—Sûrya. It is of the same plan as those at Son Kausârî, but roofed with long slabs of stone. The *pradakshina* has had a slanting roof, and two small windows at the back. One pillar of the mandap alone remains standing, with four-armed figures on the brackets. Ganes'a is carved on the lintel of the door, and Sûrya inside is represented much as Vishnu usually is, but with only two hands, and holding up a flower in each, with a nimbus behind the head, ringlets descending from behind the ears, and wearing a sort of mural crown. Beside him are three smaller figures now somewhat defaced: one of them has been a well-carved female with a mace (?) in her right hand, and her hair dressed in the style prevalent in the great S'aiva temple at Pattadkal.

A small temple in front of this has been entirely seized upon by the roots of a vad or banyan tree, which twine round the stones of the roof and walls and about the images—ten in number, each about 2½ ft. high—among whom

---

* Some groups photographed.
† Plan and three photographs taken.

are Ganpati and several female figures—one a horse-headed kinnara—all in a sitting posture, but much worn by time. The Sûrya Wâv, on the east side of this, is also overgrown by a banyan tree.

Gop.

February 15th.—At Nânâ Gop or Junâ Gop, to the south-east of Gop Hill, there is a large cavern which has been occupied by ascetics: and on visiting it I discovered in the village the shrine of an old temple, perhaps the only fragment now standing of the old city, which appears to have covered a considerable area round the present village. This shrine seems to have been last used as one of the towers of a small fort, the east and south curtain walls of which have been built of the stones of the temple that once surrounded this shrine : for in this ancient type of temple the shrine occupied almost the centre of the building, and was surrounded by a double court,—the outer one a few feet lower than the inner one and shrine.* The shrine itself is 10 ft. 9 in. square inside and about 23 ft. high, with walls 2 ft. 6 in. thick, built of coursed ashlar, each course about 8 in. deep and carefully jointed. At 11 feet from the floor are four holes in the back and front walls, each 14 in. high, as if for joists, and over them in the side walls are six smaller ones, as if for rafters. For 6½ feet above this the walls are perpendicular, then the area contracts, as in the temples of Son Kansârí ; six or seven courses having bevelled edges, but those above them square faces, until the apex is covered by a single slab.

Part of the front wall over the door has fallen and been rebuilt, but with the inner sides of the stones turned out, showing the sockets of the clamps with which the stones had been secured.

On the left jamb of the door is carved the line :—

It is not easy to say what may be the age of these letters : but I feel inclined to regard the building as the oldest structure of the kind in Kâthiawâd, and probably not later than the sixth century,—how much older I am not at present prepared to say.

Inside are two figures in yellow stone, to which the villagers give the names of Râma and Lakshmana,†—Râma with a high square *mukuta*, and Lakshmana with a low crown, long ears, ringlets, and holding a spear in his right hand.

On the fragments of the basement that remain, are many curious old dwarf-figures like the *gana* we find on the Caves of Badâmi, and on the old Vaishnava temple at Aiholli ; but the stone is very much weather-worn.

---

* Photographed from the east, south, and from the top of the round tower forming the north-west bastion of the fort. Sketch made of the roof, and measurements taken for a plan.
† Photographed.

n 197—c

The roof is quite peculiar, being a hipped stone one, pierced with two chaitya-window arches on each side,[*] which have all originally contained figures. Ganpati is still in one on the west side, and another *Deva* occupies one on the north.

The inner court has been 35 ft. 2 in. square. with a bay on the east side, 18 ft. 4 in. by 7 ft. 3 in. The outer court must have been about 9½ ft. wide.

JAMNAGAR.

19th February.—This town being of quite recent origin there is not much of antiquarian interest about it. At the village of Nâgnâ, close by, are some old temples, but no way noteworthy, and many monumental pâliyas.

The front of the palace[†] and the Dehli Gate[†] of the town, both built by the Jâm Ranmalji, about forty years ago, are fair specimens of modern Hindu architecture. So also is the temple of Vishnu in course of erection by the Diwan—the ' Dives ' of the town—and which, curiously enough, was mentioned in the last report of the district as a dharmas'âlâ—a work of general public utility. A set of six images of black marble—Vishnu or Krishna, Garuda, Sathbhâmâ, Lakshmi, Jambuvati, and Râdhâ[‡]—are ready for installation as soon as the temple is completed.

A Nanakpanthi ascetic, who dresses in silks and satins, is one of the lions of the place : he is physically a magnificent man. S'âktism is secretly practised here.

KACHH.

22nd February.—The town of Mundra has been largely built of the stones of the old city of Bhadres'var, about twelve miles north-east from it. It contains little of note except a dome[‡] or *chattri* over the *pâdukâ* or foot-prints of a Jaina high-priest of the Achalagachha, § 13½ feet square inside, with a small *s'ikhara* [¶] over the *pâdukâ*. Round them is an inscription given in the Appendix to *Memorandum No. 2.* The interior of the dome is neatly carved·with standing musicians at intervals, as is usual in Jaina domes. Near it is a pâliya with a ship carved on it, indicating that the person to whose memory it is erected, was a seafarer.

At Barai, about a mile from Mundra, is a temple of Nilakantha Mahadeva or S'iva of the blue-neck enclosed in a small court. And at the right side of the shrine door is an inscription given in *Memorandum No. 2* : it is dated in Samvat 1724 =A.D. 1667. The *linga*, which is over-shadowed by a large seven-headed brass snake, is said to have been brought from the temple of Dudhâ at Bhadres'var.

---

[*] Sketched.
[†] Both photographed.
[‡] Photographed.
[§] The four *gachhas* of the Jains about Mundra are the Achala, Tapa, Sola, and Khartaragachhas.
[¶] A sketch made of it.

BHADRES'VAR.

24th February.—The site of the ancient city of Bhadres'var or Bhadrâvati extends to a very considerable distance east of the present village, but most of the area has been dug over for building stone, and we may legitimately infer that, before this trenching up of the foundations was begun, many buildings above ground had been carried off. What now remains are the Jaina temple, the pillars, and part of the dome of the S'aiva temple of Dudhâ, the wâv or well close by it, two masjids—one near the shore almost buried, the dargah of Pir Lâl Shobhâ, and a fragment of the temple of Asbâpura.

With reference to the history of this place, the following is the substance of a narrative furnished by Gorji Hiravijdyaji Guru Devavijaya from the historical accounts written by his grandfather Guru Bantvijaya. The chronology is quite untenable, but further information might possibly enable us to rectify this : a complete copy of the papers might be of interest. The abridgment runs thus :—

After Râja Siddhasen's coronation at the port of Bhadrâvati on Thursday, the 5th of Chaitra S'uddh, in the twelfth year of tho Virat era, his spiritual guide Gokh Sûris'var came and stayed with him to pass the four rainy months, and instructed him in the precepts of his religion, which led to his commencing, in the twenty-second year of the Virat era, the building of a temple to be dedicated to a god which he named Vasâi.

Râja Siddhasen was descended from Hari, and reigned for 68 years.

In the eightieth year of the Virat era, Mahâsen, his son, succeeded him, and ruled for 53 years.

Narasen, the son of Mahâsen, then ascended the throne in 133 Virat, and reigned for 91 years. He took care of tho temple of Vasâi.

His son Bhojrâja next ascended the throne in 244 Virat, and ruled for 36 years. He caused the temple to be repaired.

His contemporary sovereign in Marwar was Râja Samvrati, who professed Jain religion and built both in his own country and throughout India 125,000 Jaina temples. When he visited Bhadrâvati he dedicated to, and placed over the Vasâi idol elephants carved in stone.

Bhojrâja having no male offspring, his brother's son, Vanrâja, succeeded him in 260 Virat. Vanrâja was a powerful monarch, and caused repairs to be made in the temple. His reign extended over a period of 59 years.

His son Sârangdeva was after him crowned king in 319 Virat, and reigned for 62 years.

His son Virsen, who was next placed on the throne, 381 Virat, conducted the government for 40 years.

Harisen, his son, was then seated on the throne, 421 Virat, and held the reins of government for 35 years. He was zealously attached to the Jain religion. He was truthful, and his mind was bent on the impartial dispensation of justice.

This ruler had no male issue, and, therefore, his widow Lilávati with the assistance of her excellent prime-minister for five years conducted the administration of political affairs. In the meantime of the two sons of Gandharva Sen, the sovereign of Malwa, Bhartrihara and Vikrama, the former becoming the rightful heir to the throne, the latter got displeased and left the country. Whereupon Bhartrihara abdicated the throne and retired from public life, when Vikrama, in his absence, returned and ascended to the throne.

Vikram became a very powerful monarch. He conquered kingdoms in different parts of the country, subjected them to his sway, and then made them over to their former masters. In the course of these conquests he appeared before Bhadrávatî, took it, and then resigned it to Lilávatí, the widow of Harisen, who thereafter reigned for 27 years.

It was at this time that Rája Vikram organized the system of castes; and in the year 470, causing the discontinuance of the Virat era, established his own, which he called "Samvat Vir Kshaya", (i.e., the era which put a stop to the Virat era). From this time the Samvat of Vikram dates its commencement.

In the eleventh year of the Samvat of Rája Vikram, Queen Lilávatí during her lifetime resigned the reins of government to Kirtidhar, a nephew of Rája Harisen, who enjoyed the blessings of the reign for 79 years.

Dharnipál, his son, ascended the throne after him in Samvat 90, and reigned for 42 years. He and his father Kirtidhar extended favourable encouragement to the Jain religion. By their performance of solemn, sacred, sacrificial rites they raised the importance of that religion.

Rája Dharnipál's son, Devadatta, assumed after him the reins of government, Samvat 132, and ruled for 81 years. Under his administration there sprung up different principalities in different places. Accordingly Wághela Vanarája of Mujpur (taking advantage of this circumstance) appeared before Bhadrávatî in Samvat 213, conquered it, and ruled for 57 years. He likewise belonged to the Jaina religion, and extending, therefore, encouragement to the Vasái Temple caused repairs to be made therein.

His son Rája Jográja succeeded him, Samvat 270, and reigned for 80 years. Under his administration he performed many deeds of charity.

Suaditya, his son, succeeded him, Samvat 350, and reigned for 54 years.

His son Vijayaráo succeeded him, Samvat 404, and ruled for 61 years. In his reign the kingdom being shattered into fragments, there arrived on the death of Vijayaráo, in Samvat 463, Káthis from Pavagadh who made themselves masters of Bhadrávatî. Their descendants occupied the throne for 147 years.

Subsequent to these events, Samvat 618, Chaudá Kanak of Pattan came and subjugated the kingdom and governed it for 52 years. He completely repaired the temple, removing thereby all traces of antiquity, and seated therein an image of Bhagván.

Chaudá Ukkad was after him crowned king, Samvat 670. He professed the S'aiva religion. Since he was zealously attached to it he entrusted the government to his prime-minister and devoted himself to asceticism and the duties of piety and devotion. On a particular day, however, he held a levée and observed how the minister had administered the state affairs ; if his conduct was found faulty he was removed and another appointed in his stead.

In this manner 700 prime-ministers were changed, and at length, finding none managing the affairs satisfactorily, he nominated a Mughul to the prime-minister-ship. Even this minister's conduct was represented by the merchants to be faulty, and his life was accordingly taken away. He then took upon himself the government of the country. Entertaining hostile feelings towards the Musalmans, he daily put one of them to death.

To avenge this hatred which he bore towards them, the Musalmans invaded the place, but the invading force was annihilated. It was followed by another army from Irán under the command of Sayyid Lalsháh. Akkad Rája got this Commander treacherously buried in a pit, which put the rest of his men to flight, and thus the defeat of the army was accomplished.

Shortly after, two Muhammadan brothers, commonly known as Auliyás (i.e., simple-minded men, who were indifferent to all worldly pomp and greatness and bent upon relieving human complaints), conquered the said Rája Akkad, and from that day the Muhammadan power increased. A mausoleum for the slain Sayyid Lalsháh and other tombs were at this time built.

In honour of the distinguished slain certain fairs are held up to this day, when their tombs are visited by pilgrims. In Samvat 747 one thousand pillared mosques were erected.

Akkad Rája reigned for 77 years, and was succeeded by his son Bhavad, Samvat 747, who ruled for 51 years.

Under his government the state affairs were in a disordered condition. On his death the Solanki Rajputs of Bhangadh came and conquered the king-dom, Samvat 798, when the name Bhadrávatí was changed into Bhadres'var, by which name it still continues to be called.

These Solankis professed the Jain religion, and the first of their kings reigned for four years. Afterwards, in Samvat 802,* one Muláraja, of the Solanki line, ascended the throne and governed the state for 59 years. The following are the names of his successors : —

							Years.
1. Chámund	...	...	...	...	...	...	13
2. Durlabha	...	...	...	...	...	...	11
3. Walabha	...	...	...	...	...	...	69
4. Bhimaráo	...	...	...	...	...	...	11
5. Karnaráo	...	...	...	...	...	...	43
6. Jaymaíñha Deva	...	...	...	...	...	...	50
7. Ajayapála	...	...	...	...	...	...	33
8. Muláraja	...	...	...	...	...	...	3
9. Visaldeva	...	...	...	...	...	...	22
10. Bhimráo	...	...	...	...	...	...	8

* This date is nearly two centuries too early : see the list given below from the best information we have as yet. It is curious to find Kamárapala omitted from this one.

B—197 d

Subsequently, Bhimráo's son, Naughan, of the Solanki race, filled the throne,
Samvat 1124, and reigned for 65 years. During his administration the king-
dom was split into fragments and infested by robbers and plunderers. An army
was consequently required to be raised under the care of Visâ S'rimâli Bania
of the name of Sholâ, who supplied it with provisions, clothes, and money. In
lieu thereof the râja conveyed to him by a writing the enjoyment of a girâs,
when all the affairs in connection with it were transacted by Sholâ for 27 years,
and after him by his descendants—Hiras'â Popats'â and Sonas'â—for 33 years.
Eventually in Samvat 1182 one Jagdevas'â, who became a very distinguished merchant, received Bhadres'var in his charge from Râja Naughan,
from whom he obtained a charter which transferred to him in absolute right of
enjoyment for ever, or so long as the sun and moon continued to revolve.
Jagdus'â caused the Vasâi Temple to be repaired on an extensive scale, removing
thereby all traces of antiquity, and the form of worship therein observed was
after the Jain religion. In his time there arrived a religious instructor of that
faith, named Deva Suri, who apprised him of an approaching famine, at the commencement of the new century, that was to last for twelve years, and told him
that if he made a liberal distribution of food he would earn a great reputation.
In conformity with this instruction he sent for grain from different countries and
stored it up. In Samvat 1204 (A.D. 1148) the predicted famine commenced and
lasted up to Samvat 1215.

Men suffered many evils ; even sovereigns sought grain from Jagdus'â and
lived upon it. The merchant granted it with an unsparing hand. Subsequently,
in Samvat 1215, among a large concourse of people dining at the merchant's
house, there appeared one person who sat and continued eating for a long time.
When he had eaten to satiety he identified himself with the famine of the 15th
year, and declared that he would never now return. So saying he went his way,
and this then became well known over the land.

Jagdus'â had retained Wâghela Naughan in his service, who conducted the
administration, and at last this distinguished merchant in Samvat 1238 breathed
his last. He had no male issue, and consequently Wâghela Naughan and his
vakils—Ajarâmal Sântidâs and Nagindâs—managed the affairs. One of them,
Nagindâs, visited Pattan and returned along with the pilgrims who accompanied
the Dasa S'rîmâli Bania—Vastupâla Tejpâla, a kârbhâri of the sovereign of that
place, to Bhadres'var. The pilgrims were hospitably and so well entertained by
Wâghela Naughan that the kârbhâri on his returning home, Samvat 1286,
managed to get Sârangdeva, a grandson of Naughan, married to the daughter of
Viradhaval, the sovereign of Pattan (A.D. 1214—1243). Wâghelas and Banias
thus conjointly wielded the government of the country, thus :—

Banias.		Wâghelas.		Years.
Ajarâmal	...	Naughan	...	48
Sântidâs	...	Bhojrâja	...	43
Nagindâs	...	Sârangdeva	...	16

Of these the last-mentioned rulers, Nagindâs and Wâghela Sârangdeva,
instituted at Vasâi a sadâvrit—a permanent establishment for the dispensation
of alms to the poor, and greatly promoted the influence of the Jain religion by

their performance of highly charitable acts. It was under their administration that a Bania, Uja Adanja, who came on a pilgrimage to Vasâi, built a large temple; his sister Boladi also erected another.

Jám Halla Gajanji visited Bhadrâvâtí with the object of treacherously putting the Wâghelas and Banias simultaneously to death, but finding no opportunity to accomplish his aim, he was ultimately expelled by the Wâghelas, when he sought refuge in Vijan. Notwithstanding this, Wâghela Sârangdeva, entertaining great anxiety for the Vasâi Temple, spent all his accumulated wealth in dispensing alms, and entrusted the conduct of the ecclesiastical functions of the temple to a high-priest under the title of a "Gothi". Jam Harbhamji at this time returned from Vijan, and founded in the vicinity of Bhadres'var a town of the name of Pâvadialu. The following table gives the names of the high-priests, or "Gothis" as they came to be designated, who officiated at the temple, and the years during which they continued in office :—

		Years.
Gothi Karsandas	... ...	32
„ Snudarji	... ...	41
„ Walji	... ...	52
„ Niyâlchand	... ...	24
„ Sântidâs	... ...	31
„ Motichand	... ...	35
„ S'ivo	... ...	29

These were the ministers of the temple, and after them Gothi Pitâmbardâs was invested with the sacerdotal power, Samvat 1581. He officiated for thirteen years. During the time he continued in office the administration of state affairs was not satisfactory. Everywhere rebellions broke out. It was now that the Jâdâ race rose to eminence, and a dissension ensued between the Râo Khengarji and Jâm Râwal. The Râo with the assistance of the sovereign of Ahmedâbâd entered Kachh, when the Jâm marching from the town of Pâvadialu subdued Bhadres'var and defended it with troops.

Gothi Pitâmbardâs prayed him that he might receive the temple under his protection. Jâm Râwal assured him he might at ease perform his service at the temple. The valour of Râo Khengarji struck Jâm Râwal, a descendant of Jâm Harbhamji, with confusion. He then sought the advice of a spiritual guide, A'nand Vimal Sûris'var, who had come hither concerning his future interests. He was advised to proceeded to Hâlar and conquer the reigning Jethwâ family. Actuated by this advice he set out by a sâtmargi way (i.e., a way having seven branches). At his departure he placed twelve of the Bhadres'var Chovisi towns—Hatdee, Pavdialo, Bharodio, Badko, Kukadsar, Wadalo, Luni, Kuva, Ranupadar, Chokhando, Wowar, Bhadres'ar—in dharmâda under the temple, and granted other 85, in all 97 towns, in dharmâda to other people.

He reached Hâlar, and subjected to his sway the country ruled by the Jethwâ family. He founded in Samvat 1596 a town in Hâlar, while Râo Khengarji founded Bhuj in 1506.

The twelve towns of Bhadres'var Chovisi which Jâm Râwal, as above stated, granted in dharmâda to the temple under the ecclesiastical government of a

Jaina religious instructor A'nand Vimal Sûris'war and Gothi Pitâmbardâs were now by Râo Khengarji, in order to immortalize his name, by a lekh conveyed in perpetuity, as if by absolute sale, to the religious instructor A'nand Vimal Sûris'war. From this date the towns are declared as so granted in perpetuity. The religious teacher A'nand Vimal Sûris'war and Gothi Pitâmbar having resigned their office, the administration of the affairs of the temple devolved in Samvat 1606 upon Vijâya Danasûri and Gothi Prâgji, who officiated for 23 years, and the following are the names of their successors:—

		Years.
Vjayahirasuri	Gothi Narsing	23
Sensuri	Velji	24

A religious instructor Kirtivijaya and his disciple Vivakeharkh succeeded those in office, Samvat 1653, and as proprietors of the jâgh'r discharged their sacredotal functions. It was in their time that Hâla Dungarji murdered a brother-in-law of Jâm Wibhâji of Nagar, Samvat 1642, by whom he was consequently banished the country. He removed his moveables and went to Gundiâli, but being a murderer his Bhâyads lent him no assistance. He presented himself thereupon before Râo Bhârmalji, who was his maternal brother, and begged him to procure Bhadres'var for him. The Râo in reply told him that a jâghir granted in dharmâda, and tolerably well managed, could not be made over to him. On hearing this he departed, went to Bhadres'var, and made himself master of the fort.

Gorji Vivakeharkh and Gothi Velji laid a complaint before the Râo, but no arrangement could be settled. The matters were then formally represented to the sovereign of Ahmedâbâd, and his assistance was solicited. From him a pariwâna was obtained, which advised that assistance be rendered in the cause of charity. It was laid before the Râo, but the Bhadres'var Chovisi towns were not placed under Vasâi ; only the following four towns—Kukardi, Ch'hasarâ, Chokhâ and Bagdâ—were given in dharmâda.

The Râo then came to Bhadres'var, Samvat 1659, re-took the fort from Dungarji, directed him to build another town in Ghorwâdâ in the suburbs, gave him out of the Bhadres'var girâs 500 prajns of land, and re-established his own jurisdiction over the place.

Even Dungarji on this occasion placed four fields under the Vasâi Temple in dharmâda.

On the death of Gothi Velji, the high-priest of Vasâi, the guardianship of the temple came to be entrusted to Gothis Moti, Hira, Naima, and Râma. These for 106 years watched over the interests of the jâghir, when, Samvat 1665, in the time of Purushrâm an army of Mosum Beg entered and considerably devastated it. Bhadres'var was plundered, the idols of the temple were mutilated, and there was a general flight of the people.

Gothi Ráma died in 1784 and Gothi Manordás succeeded him as the guardian of the jághir. He continued in office for 16 years. Gothi Bagwandás succeeded him in Samvat 1800, and officiated for 32 years. He could not efficiently watch the interests entrusted to his care, so that before the appearance of the army of Balaudkhán, Kukardi and other possessions had severed their connection with Vasái.

.Gorji Kranti Vijayaji on personally representing the state of things to the Ráo at Bhuj, an arrangement was secured for the restoration of the lost girás.

Now, Samvat 1817, Hálá Dungarji's brother, Kubarji, who was received by Thakur Punja, a kárbhári of Ráo Ghodeji, in his service, accompanied his master to Hálas, when the latter was disturbed by the Ráo. Kubarji's girás passed on this occasion into the hands of the Darbár, while Dungarji's descendants continue in the enjoyment of their own.

The Hálás now began dismantling the walls, &c., of the fort, a circumstance which gave rise to a tumult in which Gothi Ráma was slain. His brother Gothi Bhagwandás having complained to the Bhuj Darbár concerning those proceedings, Samvat 1820, or A.D. 1764, three sawárs and 50 footmen were sent as másals on them. Notwithstanding this, their men on their behalf and the people in the neighbourhood carried away the stones from the temple and ruined buildings. Among others one Jethá, who was a mehtá of those Hálás, built of these stones a dwelling-house for a gosain and a temple in the town.

Vasái, being thus reduced to this evil state, Gorji Khantvijayaji undertook in Samvat 1862 to protect its interests; and all the repairs that were made till Samvat 1907 (A.D. 1841) cost Rs. 17,000. From Samvat 1907 the temples have been closed, and the Banias at the advice of Gorji Khantvijayaji have employed a Rájgarh Raghanath, by whom they get the usual rites of worship performed.

The chronology of the above is very loose : the list of the Pattan Solankis and Wáhgelas stands thus :—

Muláréja	...	...Samvat	998-1053 = 55 years.
Chámund	...	... „	1053-1066 = 12¼ „
Valabha	...	... „	6 months.
Durlabha	...	„	1066-1077 = 11 years.
Bhima Rája	...	„	1077-1129 = 52 „
Karna Rája or Visaldeva	„	1129-1149 = 20 „
Jayasiñhadeva...	...	„	1149-1198 = 49 „
Kumárapála	...	„	1198-1229 = 31 „
Ajayapála	...	„	1229-1232 = 3 „
Muláréja II.	...	„	1232-1234 = 2 „
Bhimadeva II...	...	„	1234-1270 = 36 „
Vria Dhaval Waghela	„	(?) 1300	(?)
Visal Deva	...	„	1300-1318 = 18 „
Arjundeva	...	„	1318-1331 = 13 „
Sárangdeva	...	„	1331-1335 = 4 „
Laghu Karna ...	...	„	1335-1360 = 25 „

The Dudhá Wáv has been a large and substantial one, without much architectural ornamentation about it. Over it is a lintel 17 ft. 7 in. long by 2 ft.

1 in. square. Many of the stones, however, have been carried off for building purposes.

The dome of the Dudhâ Temple that still stands is 15 ft. 8½ in. over all ; the pillars are 1 ft. 4 in. square.*

The old temple of Vasâi or Jagdus'a, as the Jaina shrine is called, is the work of several ages : it has been restored and altered no one knows how often.

The shrine is, perhaps, the oldest of all ; the spire is a comparatively recent erection ; the two outer wings can hardly be very old ; the arches put in to support broken lintels in the corridors, &c., are perhaps of the same age ; and the outside porch in front is quite recent.†

The general plan is similar to that of the Jaina temples at Delwâdâ on Mount Abu. It stands in a court about 48 ft. wide by 85 ft. in length, round which runs a corridor in front of the cells or small shrines, about 44 in number, nine of them in the back end, where the corridor has a double row of pillars. The temple is placed towards the back of this, and from the line of the front of the temple the court is covered by three domes supported by pillars. Over the porch is another large dome. Behind the cells on the left side is a row of chambers, and at the south-west corner are others, some of which at least have been used as places for the concealment of images, &c.

There are other chambers below them, entered by lifting up flagstones in the floor : on occasions of danger from Muhammadans or others the idols were buriedly deposited in these vaults, and sand thrown in after them to the level of the floor.

In the shrine are three images of white marble ; the central one—not at all large—is Ajitantha, the second of the Tîrthaṅkaras, and has carved on it the figures १२२, probably for 1622=A.D. 1566. On his right is Pârs'wanâtha with the snakehood marked s. 1232, and on his left Sântinâtha, the sixteenth Tîrthaṅkara, also marked s. 1232, or A.D. 1176. On the back wall, round the central figure, are *Kausagujas*, indicative from their position that the shrine was once occupied by a large image. On the extreme right is an image of the black or Sâmtâ Pârs'wanâtha. On the belt of sculpture which is immediately above the base, having a Devi on each principal face, there are on each side the Devi and on all the smaller facets a pair of small figures, mostly in obscene attitudes : this is not at all usual in Jaina temples.

A ground-plan was made of this large temple, and drawings of several details. Copies of the inscriptions are also given in No. 2.

South from this temple are the remains of a large mosque nearly buried in the sand. It has been built of large blocks of stone with pillars square at the base, octagon in the middle, and circular above, having bracket capitals, and supporting massive lintels 9 feet long. In front of the mehrab are two rows of columns undisturbed ; of the next two rows little remains ; then there has been

---

* A small photograph taken.

† The temple was photographed from the south, north-east, and north-west ; some small photographs of details were also taken.

a wall, and outside it other four lines of columns; and beyond them are some others, probably belonging to the porch.

Pir Lál Shobah's place has a round dome on eight pillars set against the walls : outside, however, this dome is a square pyramid, and contracts upwards by steps.

The roof of the porch is flat and divided into 9 x 3 small squares, each with a lotus flower inside. Round the architrave, above the vine-ornamented wall-head course, is a deep line of Arabic inscription in square Kufic characters. There are two lines of this on the right-end wall. The mehrab is a plain semi-circular recess without any sculpture about it. The building stands in a small enclosure formed by a rough rubble wall built on the more solid foundation of the original court wall. In this court are some graves with inscriptions in the square Kufic character.

South-west from this last is another mosque, now entered from the north side ; but the original entrance is on the east side, within which is built a small chamber, apparently never finished. The porch is raised on eight elegant pillars* with pilasters against the walls. At the back is a mehrab—a plain semicircular recess—and two neat doors leading into an inner apartment,—possibly a second place of prayer for a select number.

It has four doors, two at each end. This mosque is built of pretty large stones most accurately jointed, and all the roofs are of flat slabs. The doors have drips over them, and the two into the front apartment have semicircular arches ; the others, lintels. The architraves are carved with neat reli or creeper patterns and with large flowers below, where the Jains employ human forms.

BHUVAD, 2nd March.—The temple of Bhavânes'vara Mahádeva here is much ruined—the roof of the shrine having entirely fallen in. The mandap measures 31¾ ft. by 39¼ inside, and is supported by 3¼ pillars and 4 pilasters—18 on the screen wall and 12 of them round the dome, which covers 22 feet 9 inches square inside the columns. The pillars are square to about one-third their height, then octagon, and lastly round. The shrine has been a large one, fully 23 ft. square, domed on twelve pilasters 18 in. by 12 in., with four-armed figures on the brackets. The brackets of the columns of the mandap are plain, but a plinth of 9 or 10 in. deep above the bracket is carved with a raised geometrical pattern. The fronts of the brackets are also carved as in those of the Bhadres'var Temple.

There is an inscription on the pilaster to the right of the shrine door, dated s. 1346=A.D. 1289-90, but of the 20 lines of which it consisted only a few letters here and there can be read : it is given in No. 2.

The temple has been built of stones the whole thickness of the walls.

Over the shrine door is a Devi, probably Bhavání.

5th March.—ANJAR. In this town the temple of Mádhavráo is a Vaishnava shrine with a domed mandap, the floor laid with black and white marble. The image is of black marble decked out in petticoats, like a child's doll, and placed on a table overlaid with silver, under which is the image of Garuda. The shrine doors

---

* Drawn.

are also plated with silver, and bear an inscription by the donor dated in 1869 A.D.
On some of the eight pilasters that support the dome are carved mermaids and
nága figures.   There is also a fountain in the middle of the floor, but the pipe is
out of order.

Mohanráï's Temple is smaller and plainer, with a neatly carved wooden door.
It is also a Vaishnava shrine, the idols being Krishna, with Rádhá on his left
and Chatturbhuj—the four-armed Vishnu—on his right, small paltry images that
would not pass as good dolls.   This temple was rebuilt some 50 or 60 years ago.

Ambá Mátá's Temple and the adjoining math or monastery are built of fragments of older temples.   To a room over the gateway of the enclosure is a door
of hard reddish stone, carved all round,* which, from the repetition of Deví on the
jambs and lintel, may have belonged to a Vaishnava or S'ákta temple; sculptured
slabs also lie about, and are built into the walls.   The math belongs to the Atíts
of Ajaipála.

Ajaipála's place is outside the walls, and is a small modern-domed room,
with images of Ajaipála on horseback, and of Ganpati—both well smeared with
red paint.   At the door are two inscriptions dated in A.D. 1842 ; but the Atíts,
who wear pagdís of brick-red colour, and have a good revenue from the state,
could not give much information respecting their patron saint, whom they worship, except that he was a Chauhán king of Ajmer, who abdicated his throne,
became an ascetic, and ended his days as a samádi by a voluntary death.

They are a S'aiva sect, and the Nandi, or sacred bull, with brass horns occupies
a prominent point on the platform facing the door of the shrine.

Their pírs or gurus are buried around, and the chattris, or smalls cells, over
their remains are marked by the linga.

Jaisal was a Jádeja Rájput of Kedáná, near Tuná, who with his wife Turí
Káthiáná gave themselves up to a voluntary death about four hundred years ago,
and like Ajaipála they now enjoy divine honours.

Their shrine is a small tile-roofed room with Musalman-like tombs in it of
Jaisal, Turí and a Banya devotee.   Round the place are a number of small
chattris over páliyas.   This shrine has also an allowance from the Darbár.

It would be of interest if some one who has opportunity would investigate
the history and peculiarities of these Atíts of Ajaipála and Jaisal.

Klanes'vara Mátá's Temple is also outside the walls, and is comparatively
modern, with a dancing yoginí as its goddess.   In front of the Nandi is a tortoise.

Wankal Mátá, on the north-east of the town, is also dedicated to a form of
Bahaváni.

Bades'vara is at some distance to the south-east of the town : the shrine and
s'ikhar are probably old, but it has been repaired, and the mandap rebuilt in recent times.   On the withdrawn faces round the shrine is carved the lion-bodied
figure remarked elsewhere, but here with a considerable diversity of heads—in
this differing from those on Muni Báwás'.

---

* Drawn.

On the west of the town a new temple is being built to Dwârkanâth, and close to it is an unfinished one to Bahucherâji, with three shrines on as many sides of the intended maṇḍap. Bahucherâji is the "looking-glass" goddess, before whom the votary worships his own image in a piece of silvered glass. This is practical Hinduism, groping in childish superstition in spite of the beautiful moral maxims that are to be found in Sanskrit literature.

The other two shrines are dedicated to Bhavânî and the Linga.

BHUJ.

March 9th.—The mosque inside the gate of the city is remarkable for the thickness and closeness of the piers, of which there are four lines, each 3 ft. 10 in. by 5 ft. 5 in. to 5 ft. 11 in., separated by aisles 1 ft. 10 in. wide, except the central one, which is 3 ft. 2 in. wide. The bays are 9 ft. 3 in. wide by 46 ft. 4 in.—the length of the building inside.

Beyond the Residency are the mausolea of the Râos of Kachh. The older ones are chattris, but most of them were more or less damaged by the earth-quake in 1819, and no attempt seems to be ever made to repair any tomb that is going to ruin. Râo Lâkhaji's is the largest and finest. It was built about 1770, but, like the older one behind it, it is going to ruin, the south porch having fallen. The central dome covers an apartment surrounded by a wall with a door on the east. Across the floor of this is a line of sati stones,—Râo Lâkhâ being represented on horseback in the centre with seven *satis* on the left and eight on the right. On the twelve pillars of this dome are dancing females, and on one a mermaid,* all about 5 ft. high, and at the entrance are two chobdars. On the capitals are smaller figures, musicians, &c., about 3 ft. high, including their supports, but some of these are damaged.† Since sati was given up, the Râos are denied the honour of a chattri on their tombs.

There are a number of shrines and Musalman darghas, &c., about Bhuj, but nothing of great age or specially deserving of notice.

11th March. KERA.—At this place, about 13 miles south of Bhuj, is an old S'aiva temple, of perhaps the end of the tenth century, thrown down by the earthquake of 1819. The shrine‡ still stands, and measures 8 ft. 6 in. square inside, with walls 2 ft. 7 in. thick, surrounded by a *pradakshina* 2 ft. 6 in. wide : the vimana measuring 24 ft. over all. This temple has been built partly of red and partly of a yellowish stone, very hard, and standing exposure very well. Of the maṇḍap, which was 18 ft. 9 in. wide, only a part of the north wall with one window in it is left : all the rest lies a heap of ruins, and the amlas'ila of the s'ikhar lies outside—a block about 6 ft. in diameter.

The sculpture on the walls has been superior to the usual run of such work,§ and the ornamental work on the spire has been largely undercut : it represents the outlines of a chaitya window repeated with human figures between.

To the south-east of Kedâ is a small village on a rising ground, above which is the place of Pir Ghulam Ali. It is surrounded by trees, and there are few

* Sketched.
† A photograph was taken of this tomb with those in the vicinity of it.
‡ Photographed both from the east and west.
§ Some specimens sketched.

B 197—f

prettier places than this perhaps in Kachh. The principal buildings within the enclosure are—1, the dargah, facing the east, with one large dome, and in front of it three smaller ones. Inside is the tomb under a canopy supported by twelve small columns of the usual Muhammadan style. Against the pall lies the photograph of a Mughul pír, a water-colour portrait of Ali, with a *nimbus* round his head, and below him Hasan and Husain, also with aureoles ; and in a third frame Muhammad in a blue chogah, but the face left blank,—a curious compromise between the prohibition in the Qoran (Surah, V. 92) and the desire for a palpable representation of the objects of reverence. Looking-glasses, glass balls of all colours, cloth-parrots that look like purses, &c. &c., are hung up as votive offering. The verandah or vestibule is 28 ft. long inside, and the doors of copper bronze. 2nd, a canopy or chattra in front of the dargah, with a flat roof and balconies on each side, stands in the middle of the quadrangle. 3rd, Dâdi Ali Shâh's Dargah or cenotaph has lantern minarets, and is a neat plain building with three doors in front and two in the east end. The roof is supported by two arches the whole width of the building. It contains no tomb, the body having been buried in Irân. The doors of both the dargahs have the projecting shield between floral ornamentation found at Mahijl Sahiba's tomb at Junâgarh and on the palace, &c., at Jâmnagar. The windows are of pierced stone, the patterns being very simple ones, and all well white-washed.

The buildings were erected about 80 years ago, Ghulam Ali Shâh having died at Kurrachee about 1792. He was a Persian, and the estate attached to this establishment is said to yield 50,000 koris, or between 18,000 and 19,000 rupees, which is distributed in charity, &c.

KOTAI.

15th March.—From Kedâ I had to return by Bhuj, from which marching northwards to the shores of the Ran I came to Kotâi, where are the remains of an old city with several ruined temples of perhaps the earlier part of the tenth century. That known as Râ Lâkhâ's, ascribed to Lâkhâ Phuláni, who is said to have had his capital here, is built of the yellowish and red stone used also at Kedâ, and is roofed in a peculiar way. The aisles are covered by a sort of groins, like the side aisles in some chaitya caves ; the nave is covered in the same way as at Ambarnâth Temple, the central area being covered with massive slabs hollowed out in the centre in which a pendentive has been inserted, and outside it has a slanting roof divided into four sections of slightly different heights, that next to the spire being the highest, and the remote end the lowest : each section is terminated by a neatly-carved gable end.*

The whole has been built without any cement, and most of the stones are hollowed out on the under or inner side as if for the purpose of making them lighter.

The porch has long since fallen away. The door of the temple has been neatly carved with the nine *graha*, or patrons of the planets, over the lintels : the jambs are also carefully sculptured. In the maṇḍap are four pillars 9 ft. 4 in.

---

* Photographed.

to the top of the bracket and with a square block sculptured below the bracket, and six pilasters apparently inserted for the sake of uniformity only, for they are not of any structural use.

The shafts are 5 ft. 11 in. high, supporting a plinth 10 in. high, on which stands a block carved with colonnettes at the corners, and crowned with an amlas'ila-shaped member, the faces of the block being sculptured with figures of men and elephants. The total height is 8 ft. 5 in.

Among the four-armed figures on the brackets of the columns one is a female, and one has a face on the abdomen as at Aiholli.

In the window recesses are also pilasters with four-armed figures on the bracket capitals. The pillars and pilasters are all of the Hindu broken square form. The shrine door is elaborately carved with two rows of figures on the frieze, Ganpati on the lintel, and the jambs richly ornamented.

The area behind the central one is roofed with large slabs, carved with six-teen female figures linked in one another's arms in a circle, with the legs crossed and turned towards the centre. Each holds a rod or bar in either hand, the left hand being bent down and the right up, and so interlaced with the arms of the figures on either side. The roofs of the three aisles in front and at the sides of the central area are very prettily carved with flowered ribs, and three horizontal bands from which they spring.

In two neat gokhles, or niches, advanced from the front wall of the shrine, and with two colonnettes in front of each, there have been standing images in alto-rilievo neatly canopied by a lotus flower and buds growing over the muguts. Enormously elongated munis or bringis seem to have been the supporters.

This temple faces the west. Of the three small temples to the west of it two face the east and one the north. The last has been a very small Vaishnava temple; but only a fragment of the shrine remains. Of the middle one also only the shrine remains standing; on the walls are carved a figure of Sûrya on the west face and griffins in the recesses. Varâha has fallen off from the south wall, and there is a figure of Ganpati on the lintel—which, however, seems in Kâthin-wâd to have been used on sun temples as well as on those of S'iva. Of the third a portion of the porch as well as the shrine remains. Over the head of the shrine door are carved the nine graha. On the north wall outside is Nrisiñha, and on the west Vishnu, both much time-worn.

Across a ravine, to the north-east from this group, are fragments of two others facing west. Of the first, and higher up of the two, only two plain square pillars of the mandap and the lower part of the vimana are standing. The door is surrounded by an architrave of three members, two fasciæ carved with veli or creeper pattern and a cyma recta with leaves. The general style is the same as that of the other temples, but much plainer. On the lintel is a Ganpati, and out-side two figures much weather-worn. The stones are cut away as at the first temple.

Foundations still remain on this part of the hill, showing that whole edifices must have been carted away for building purposes elsewhere.

The lower of the two is also only a fragment of the shrine, with Gaṇpati on the lintel and the nine *graha* on the frieze. There are no figures outside.

We had now a long march along the borders of the Ran, first to Jhuran, and thence to Dudhai, near which it was officially reported there was a temple of Mâtâ Bhavâni excavated in a hill.

This turned out to be a wretchedly small natural cavern, at a considerable distance from the village, which had been appropriated as a cell for the Mâtâ, and where some bairagis stay.

At Dhamarkâ was reported " a Jaina temple of Pâra'wanâtha, built about 250 years ago." There is, indeed, a Jaina temple, such as is to be met with in almost any village where there are Banyas, but of no interest either for size or decoration, and probably not more than 80 years old.

From this I went on to Bandri, and thence to Kanthkoṭ, an old fortress on the top of an isolated rocky hill, the steep scarp of which has been crowned by a wall built of massive blocks; but it has in later times suffered severely, and been repaired or largely replaced with one of much smaller stones.

There is a portion of an old Jaina temple in this fort which had had a double *mandap*, but it is much ruined, some of the lintels having been used a century or two ago for salt stones at the old burning-ground close by. The temple has, doubtless, been a fine one, and on some of the pillars are inscriptions, only very partially legible, one of which is dated s. 133+, (i.e.) about A.D 1280. It is so situated that it would be very difficult to get a photograph of it except from a considerable distance, and the details are all too weather-worn to be made out. There is an old temple of Sûrya close by,* on which is an inscription in small characters—from position and present condition not suitable either for taking a rubbing or an éstampage of, but which might have been copied had I only had a qualified s'âstri or pandit with me.

Near a more modern shrine on the wall are a number of graves of S'aiva Atits, several of which present somewhat novel forms.

20th March.—At Kokrâ or Kakrâ, about a mile south of Kanthkoṭ, are two ruined temples, quite in the jungle, both of them S'aivite. In the more easterly one there is a fine door to the shrine, which, had time admitted, I would have made a drawing of. It is evidently old, of hard compact stone, and has a chaitya-window ornament over each jamb, and the different compartments of the lintel. On the lintel S'iva is carved in the centre, Brahma on the left, and Vishnu on the right, in a very spirited style, with kirtimukhs between. Some well-sculptured pillars also lie about.

Had time permitted I should next have proceeded to Rav and Gedi, but the season was advancing and becoming very sultry, and water was scarce and bad; besides my information had hitherto proved very unsatisfactory, and much

---

* Image sketched.

time was lost in making long excursions to find that the remains reported were of but very little interest, and at Shahpur I decided on moving towards Râdhanpur. From Shahpur the route now led by Bhimês'ar to Adis'var, whence I crossed the Raṇ to Santhalpur, and marched first to Warai and next to Râdhanpur, where I hoped to have been able to trace some copper-plates found about a year before, and said to be in excellent preservation. This I quite failed in, but it is to be hoped careful enquiry will yet be made for them, and accurate facsimiles obtained of them.

30th March.—SANKES'VAR. Though traditionally a place of great antiquity, being mentioned by Merutanga A'chârya as S'ankhpur, contains but little of note now. To the north of the village is an old inscription, much weather-worn, of which the date is doubtfully read s. 1322=A.D. 1266. It is on an upright stone, standing by itself. Over the inscription is the sun and moon, and under them a cow with a calf and a pig, in sign of a joint agreement between Hindu and Musalman. A little way from this, on the site of an old fort or town, are two carved stones;—one of them a circular slab, with three figures on it : the central one a male figure with four hands holding a chattri, and on his left is a female chauri-bearer, and on his right another female holding a cup and some other object. The sculpture is 2 ft. 3 in. in diameter, and the legs slant inward to accommodate the circular figure.

The other stone, about 3 ft. 8 in. long, is a representation of Vishṇu on S'esha, with three figures between Brahma and Lakshmî. The males have all square-topped muguts as at Badâmî, while the females have chignons.

In the village is a pretty large temple of Pârs'wanâtha, the lower part of it mostly of marble, and with a bimtî or surrounding corridor of small shrines. It was built in 1811, and is in no wise remarkable either in general style or execution of details ; and the Pardesi keeper was obstructive and annoying, as his class usually are in such places.

Near it are also the remains of an old brick Jaina temple of s. 1652= A.D. 1596, much ruined.

Outside is a neat chattri to a s'ripuja or high-priest with an inscription.*

JHINJUWADA.

13th April.—Jhinjuwâdâ, said to derive its name from a Rôbari of the name of Jhinju, was probably a border fortress of the Balhara kings of Anhillawâdâ Pattan in the twelfth century towards Saurâshṭra as was Dabhoi on their south-east frontier. The original walls formed a square of nearly half a mile on each side. In the middle of each was a gate. The Dhâmâ Gate on the north,† the Nâgawâdâ on the east, Mâdâpola on the west, and the Râkshasapola on the south,—the latter now built up. At the south-west corner is the only tower‡ of the original four now left standing, and a much smaller square than the original one has been en-

---

* Copied.
† Photographed both from the outside and from within.
‡ Rough sketch made.

closed by a wall, built by one of the Ahmedâbâd kings, with circular bastions and an arched gateway. The place is now held by a petty Koli chief.

Between the east and north gates is the old multilateral tank, about 300 yards in length and not much less in breadth, originally surrounded by a neat embankment with ghâts of steps and inclined planes at intervals ; but one side of it has entirely disappeared, and the other seems to have been much ruined since the date of Mr. K. Forbes's visit to it.

The gateways are much in the same style and of the dimensions of those at Dabhoi, but have never been so elaborately carved. Again and again on the stones are carved the letters—

महं श्री उदल.

This, Mr. K. Forbes says, "is supposed to indicate that Udayan Mantri was the minister employed in the direction of the work." I cannot see the grounds for such a supposition. Udala and Udayana are quite distinct names, and Udal is still a name among the Chârans in this part of Guzerat.

It was difficult to obtain either information or anything else at Jhinjuwâḍâ; and but for the attentive kindness and great intelligence of Muhammad Ismail, the Salt Inspector, I should have had difficulties in getting on.

The season was now oppressively hot ; we had had a severe thunder-storm at Râdhanpur, and others threatened, so it was determined to proceed towards Ahmedâbâd.

The country to the east and north-east of Jhinjuwâḍâ would probably well repay a visit, but it must be undertaken at an earlier season of the year. The Nâgwâḍâ Wâv, said to be about 8 miles east of Jhinjuwâḍâ, is reported to be a fine one ; Mudhera had one of the finest temples in Guzerat still standing, at least only five years ago, and possibly it may have still escaped the vandalism of the Gaik-wâd's people ; and there are other places round the ancient capital Anhillawâḍâ Pattan that ought at least to be enquired about.

At Ahmedabad I was unfortunate in missing the Executive Engineer, who had gone to Gogha. But I looked over the sculptured stones that had been dug out of the foundations of the old Muhammadan fort* during my tour : these stones had evidently been taken from Hindu or Jaina temples by the Musalmans. One of them bears a short inscrip-tion dated s. 1359 = A.D. 1303. Most of them, if not all, might be preserved ; but I marked a number of the more specially interesting ones, which might be sent to Bombay and placed in the museum, in accordance with Government Resolution No. 24 C. W.—45 of 8th January 1875.

* See Memorandum from Superintending Engineer, Northern Division, No. 4508 of 18th December 1874.

The inscriptions from Ahmedâbâd, of which I had obtained good rubbings in December, I took to the Photozincographic Office in Poona and had them, to-gether with a rubbing of an inscription from Girnar, carefully photozincographed to suitable scales, and a pair of copper-plates from Walleh excellently photo-graphed by Mr. Cousins. His negatives were brought home with my own, and are now at the India Office, while prints have been sent to eminent scholars, and already I have promise of translations of all those in the Arabic character.

This memorandum with the two preceding ones will indicate sufficiently the work done during the season; and the materials with those privately accumulated in former years, which I hope also to utilize, are more than amply sufficient for a much more extensive report than I can hope to prepare during my stay here.

The exact number of photographs, inscriptions, and drawings I am unable at present to state, as all the negatives and many of the inscriptions are at the India Office, and I have not, as yet, got prints from them; whilst a large number of the smaller inscriptions are included in Memorandum No. 2, of which I have not yet received a copy.

The great deficiency of the survey this season has been the want of more draughtsmen : there was ample work for three, and I had only one. This defect I trust will be remedied next season.

I have the honour to be,

Sir,

Your obedient Servant,

J. BURGESS,

Archæological Surveyor and Reporter,

on Special Duty.

BOMBAY : PRINTED AT THE GOVERNMENT CENTRAL PRESS.